# The Amnesiac's Birthday

Cemetery Dance Publications
132-B Industry Lane, Unit #7
Forest Hill, MD 21050
www.cemeterydance.com

ISBN: 978-1-58767-797-7

# The Amnesiac's Birthday

by Terri Adamczyk

CEMETERY DANCE PUBLICATIONS

Baltimore, MD
2021

*to my sister, Katherine*

# Table of Contents

# Invocation

*Be glad of any peace that leaves this center in its circle*
*safe. Yet think how every beating heart contains*
*the simple, necessary tools to pound*
*its own damnation into life, can choose tonight, tomorrow*
*night, or any ordinary day, to let its blood run cold*
*and could. Inside my head and all the strangled vessels*
*of my heart, I pray I've built no home to house*
*such bloody tenants: envy, anger, over-ripened*
*hatred that smiles while it wipes a cold machete's sharp*
*curve clean, wondering what it takes*
*to best put out an eye.*

# Foreword

by Marge Simon

When Adamczyk's editor, Norman Prentiss, asked me to take an advance look at this collection, I didn't know what to expect. I had never heard of the poet before, and hadn't exchanged messages with Norm in a while. But hey, this is Prentiss, a man whose writing and poetry skills I've long admired! I was curious—maybe her collection would be a surprise. He sent the file, I read "Invocation," and my immediate response was "This is a poet."

> ...I pray I've built no home to house
> such bloody tenants: envy, anger, over-ripened
> hatred that smiles while it wipes a cold machete's sharp
> curve clean, wondering what it takes
> to best put out an eye.
>
> —lines from "Invocation"

Never heard of Terri Adamczyk? Okay, where does a book *come* from, after all? These writers who seem to show up out of nowhere, fully formed with a mature voice—and you wonder why they haven't been published before, why they aren't already famous, haven't been "discovered" until now.

I'm reminded a bit of Woolf's essay on "Shakespeare's sister," imagining another writer as great as the famous playwright, with as rich an imagination, but circumstances didn't encourage her gifts. Further imagining, what of Mary Shelley? (You know, the Mary who wrote *Frankenstein*.) Although Shelley didn't always get due respect during her lifetime, her poor Monster is still alive and kickin' worldwide today, while her poet husband's works are generally limited to the domain of profs and scholars. Certainly, barriers are put into our lives, creative or otherwise. You don't need a hypothetical situation. It's there, you deal with it.

Ms. Adamczyk hints at her own struggles in "Invocation" and the title poem. Consider the idea that memory loss must be one of the most frightening things for a poet. You'll find a theme throughout that describes amnesia in bits and pieces:

> All amnesia's emptied cells are full of phantom
> roots and limbs on fire. Who fuels the fire? Feel
> the blisters bubbling in the emptied air. This is not
> the garden where the world is named. Here
> all names are flaming swords laid blade
> against the skin...
> —lines from "The Amnesiac's Birthday"

When Adamczyk's lines twine & twist around in your head, you can't stop to let them go; a poem wills its way through the surface of realization, neutralizes your self-protective barriers. It takes some practice, and you can't first read her poems standing up:

> But some other ill-fated voyage would go on instead,
> that ship that was trapped
> in the pack ice—trying, trying to find the way
> through the polar sea—they failed.
> But nobody died, except for the sled dogs the sailors loved;
> only slowly the growing idea
> that there weren't enough seal, enough penguins, enough food
> for men and dogs both, they swallowed their tears
> as they ate. Though all of them might have died
> without their dogs, and if somebody couldn't pull out a gun
> and dry-eyed shoot them with one shot, humanely in private. It took
> two years to cross over the polar ice. Nobody cried
> except that once for the dogs, but they cheered
> when the opening ice became the open sea,
> wild clamoring, pounding their leaky boats. Strong arms
> almost too leaden to row. Hard choices. The weakest
> can hardly bail. At the first approachable freckle
> of land, an eyebrow of rocks not sand, an unassailable cliff
> overhead, the captain is already choosing who

with their bodies failing too fast, must disembark, their lifeboats
pulled up for some cover. How can they not cry when he leaves?
But they believe, as believers do, he will bring them home.
—lines from "The Presumption of Loss"

If you haven't guessed yet, this passage refers to Shackleton's 1914 Antarctic
expedition. That last line chills to the bone, with a punch forward to imply a
larger meaning. It's like what we do to enlarge a photo on a screen. You form a
pinch and spread your fingers, voila! —enlarged and refocused. Let's spread our
fingers: Prentiss informed me that Adamczyk writes everything in longhand.
Before typewriters, poets and writers composed in longhand. I think their work,
like hers, was more carefully crafted from the start. Paper and ink were dear; you
couldn't erase, you had to scratch through a word to discard it. I'm guessing she
composes each line succinctly in her head, then works to get it down quickly, as
close to the original as possible. By writing in longhand, the poet can develop a
different kind of feel, a different appreciation of line length and word choices,
which is apparent in her work.

To quote renowned speculative poet Bruce Boston, "The best poems,
speculative or otherwise, have substance and passion, complemented by craft."
Terri Adamczyk's poetry has that in spades—through pain and ordeal, a keenly
gifted mind and an unfailing will to express. Imagine, being a poet your whole
life, knowing you're a *good* poet, but not having anything like a career, or a
published book, and fearing that the clock is ticking away. For me, this collection proves it's never too late. And how inspiring it is that there are so many
writers who persist past rejection letters or lost opportunities, keep writing, and
can end up producing a book enriched by life's struggles, turning it into art.

# I.
# In the
# House of
# Self-Undoing

# Why is it only stone

hills sprouting skeletal

trees? A Main Street of maples withholding

all leaves, tight-lipped

buds pimple twigs; it is cold,

despite crocuses practically

purple in front of Skibiski's. Sap

drains from maples and Sundays

the men empty buckets, collecting

the runoff in trucks. It is slow,

like the sap, slow, lugging buckets

from every tapped tree. Flanked by gray

aisles, rough bark, or facing

scalped fields without squash vines

or weeds, I refuse

to take root. It's a pale place

excepting the brush

fires' bursting combustible circles

of timber, explosions of orange, and lately,

forsythia splurging their pliable

stalks against rock

hills. Sugarloaf thawed,

without leaflets, is empty.

Its birches, in pine strands, gleam

gunmetal cold against yellow

and yellow

and yellow buds frothing in sleet.

## The stillborn spirit

is not unloved but put away for contemplation

when it means much more, yet feels like freezing

loss untouched. A doctor holds

an oddly swaddled baby,

offers him to me, "He's perfect.

Wholly perfect." I saw his lashes

dark above his cheeks, the lids locked shut

and blue. The doctor leans across my arm

and whispers, "Perfect."


"A perfect baby boy, but dead," I said

to people here and there along the hallway

to the grave. He's perfect, absolutely

perfect, his lips and fingers never shocked

to breathe or move. His body, just the way

it is supposed to be, except too soon and even still

he is too close to living to be buried. Only laid

like Snow White's brother in a coffin

made of glass to show the way perfection born

without its life, is not unloved, the hands

that do not curl up and close, the mouth that doesn't suckle,

appear through glass, as if to pierce one's life with loss.

Each limb is laid out gently

so his breathless body lasts as long as ours.

If only someone had the key

to free his soul locked just behind his lips.

Is that the dream, a piece of poisoned apple

stuck inside his throat? Here is the lonely
imperfection of the stillborn body,
beautiful, undamaged, dead.

## In the house of self-undoing

fear and doubts like quarried rock accumulate

as heavily as sin, yet lacking the formal grace

of penance to alleviate their weight; each one

the solid heft of it heaped on that aching pile,

hurts. Each one, a chunk of granite fieldstone flecked

with quartz, some near translucent sheets of mica,

gravel, boulders, marble slabs and slate, bereft

of just the smallest finger's choice to bear down

light or hard enough to kill, must give

itself completely to this task. A task the Inquisition

could have ordered crushing guilt from one accused,

condemned but still unable to accept

the slow temptation to confess. There must be suffering

sufficient to illuminate the shape and feel

of crimes as varied as the weights of rocks. There must be time

to probe one's whole anatomy of skin:

for every hardened, crusted kind of guilt, like scabs

torn off, the opened wounds will ooze

like evidence of error to be punished. I've been

pressed already, not by rocks alone, but thoughts (my own),

that scream like circling vultures wanting to devour

bits and pieces of the dead, and then the bleeding head.


One could confess to anyone to everything, to all and still

another rock would settle on the rest, to slow one's breath,

to speed one's thoughts that pierce like chiseled flint

through ruined skin to unexpected sin. There is
no wriggling down through softer soil that is somewhere
far below the hardpacked dirt or flagstones fitted neatly
side by side. No escape or crawling out
the way an ant can pass, as if a camel
through the needle's eye, from empty space to space
between two stones. I have no mind for that,
no art or faith in any transformation
so complete I'd lose this self, this heart,
this chest, these lungs still filled with a desire
to release this last, stale breath of air for fresh.
The mind says, "Don't." Exhale that final, bursting
breath and even this small space still holding life
will settle farther down. Press one small pebble
more, or two, atop the rest until the ribs first crack,
then break, the heart erupts, the lungs left flat
and useless as a moth's wings caught between two hands,
and crushed or pinned upon a rock. The wings are nothing
to the rock; the hands caught and felt its beating
like a captive heart, these hands indifferent
to that life left barely living, once a thumb
and fingers rub the wings into tissue
that cannot fly. I might,
searching through the depths of named
and unnamed wrongs, find somewhere marked upon me

one small scar a picked scab leaves behind, if not
the broken moth, then envy's wish to make
one's sister crumple up against the floor and cry.

Cut that scar apart, it bleeds almost enough, but not,
to satisfy the hands that know a moth should fly,
the lungs should fall and lift, the sister must be
given back her doll, the brutal names
not called. Perhaps there is no scar and this
is just the executioner who's skilled at forcing
sin and unforgiven guilt to go on pressing longer
than you'd ever think the body could sustain.
Does such an executioner exist who places
rock by rock, this fear and sharpened doubt
upon my chest? Yet no one stands behind me
with an ax or dangles swords
above my head, I look,
as often as the rocks allow,
and this is who I am, the one who wields
such weights, destroys each breath, and seeks
the unknown damage buried
in the skin. There is a rock to crush each sin,
to hold beneath each boulder, every grain
of what one wishes to have never thought or done,
but loathing can't be smashed between two rocks,
or ten. It lingers on like pus that seeps infected
from within. For this there is the weight
of rocks to force one's full confession; only
how can one confess what one forgets?

I am afraid to look below these stones more lovely
than my soul, my heart is weak,
afraid and pounding—is it worse to die, or almost die?

I have no strength to roll one pebble smaller

than a heartbeat, or a fieldstone, off myself. My arms

are frozen quartz below them. Could I be allowed

as simply as an ant to crawl away, I'd find

these broken, splintered feet can't move. If any

other hand could lift that growing granite

weight away, would this scraped and scratched

and bleeding body that exists to be destroyed

all night, all day and never done, be done—

and would it be too ugly to restore? If every rock

could burst from cold, unmoving mineral to flame

that burns away, each stone becoming

only fire's ashes, light as moth's wings blown away,

I'd see my scarred and unseen sins exist

exposed to balm and bandages enough, I might be

cured of curing all I can't confess or find

with stone on stone on stone, a task

the Inquisition could have ordered, ended.

## When First a Child

old enough to want, I wanted Rapunzel's hair,
long enough to touch the floor and thick enough
to braid into a rope. What better hair
could be imagined, unless it could be changed to black
from brown. Yet if ever once my hair grew long enough
to touch my ears, then mother said, "I see
it's time we had a haircut, short." No matter how long
or hard I cried, despite the desperate call to Father's
office, nothing saved my hair: or me,
from my mother's firm desire to foreshorten any beauty
that might be growing past her strong hands'
hold on me, my hair. I prayed to God, as good a prayer
as, "If I die before I wake, I pray the Lord
my soul to take." I added on, "Please, if I awake, allow
my hair to be like all my friends in ponytails and braids."
This prayer went every night unanswered; I could only think
God wished for me to be a boy.

Soon enough my parents had my sister
with her white-blonde hair and black, shiny
shoes for church and fluffy dresses, while I lay unneeded
like a mummy in a tomb, unseen. Painted, on the sarcophagus
the death mask is a boy. Inside, laid out, dressed for death,
the girl wrapped tight in winding cloths was growing.
In that locked, dark tomb, still life continues—until
the woman's red river ran through the girl

who should have been a boy. The mother

had to take her out, unwind the bandages,

and force herself (confused) to welcome her first daughter

back, to let her hair grow long and brown. The scissors

Mother used, put down, her boar's bristle brush untangling

my knotted hair. But the boy's face came

at night, each night, and covered the face below;

so only once a month I knew I was not a girl

who ought to be a boy, but was a girl both night and day

who should have been a girl and is.

# Found under an unused book in July,

the letter said, "Dear Daughters, know
I have always loved you. Please call
the Doctor and thank him for all his work."
I never called, and left unmailed my own letter back:

Dear Doctor,
Why is she like this, our mother? All the best parts
twisted apart and discarded, or left unused in your
office drawer. Why should she trap us in paths
between piles of papers too special to throw away?
Only one match would burn down these paper walls and letters
to the Doctor, and to death and daughters, would disappear,
as well as other letters trying to leave us behind, "Could you
take my daughters, Dear Sister, I've scarred them for life."
So many letters littered among grocery lists and errands,
what food to fix, "Love Mom." These, and her face
gone blank say, "Die, die, die." But nobody ever says
that one word, "Die." Did she want to, even after
July? Didn't she love us more than death? Did she ever say
"Die"? Did she ever say it to you? Did you send her home
to try, unsuccessfully? Can I say thank you? No. but I can
say, "Die," out loud. Did she tell you she loved us forever the best
of all? If not, at least, could you lie, if trying to die
becomes dead. But no, no, no one said, "Dead" or "Died,"
like, "Lucky she didn't die." No. The proper expression
was accident, as in "This was only an accident you know."

An accident can be survived, but you can't be sure each time
if you'll live or die, like Icarus flying too high, not the
exuberant heights, each heartbeat lifting you higher, ferocious sun
melting your flight; instead you are sinking too low, the moist,
moist water struggling to pluck your heavy wings out
of the air. Only today she was strong. Only today she didn't die.
But wingless, she lives with the hope of death, and why was I
the one bringing water, more water, more, until I was the one
who helped her wash down enough pills to drag each minute
faster, like the last rushing rapids before Niagara Falls spills
over, pounding a life into death and consuming its anguish,
the furious wish to be dead, her relentless despair, unrelenting—

the spiraling whirlpool we can't get you out of. The ambulance
men pulled you free. The hospital pumped out your water and pills
like a swimmer rescued from drowning, you wake up—the rest
of your pills intact. They fix you all up, the nurses, finding
a comb for your hair, making sure you haven't forgotten your pills
tucked neatly into your purse. Brought home (by who?),
you resemble a stranger wearing our mother's blue
bathrobe and well enough to lie, "It was only an accident
I only wanted to sleep. You needn't have cried." Crazy,
us trying to swallow our tears like a handful of pills.

Oh Father, why did you hand her that box full of reasons
to die? Oh Doctor, why did you let her try? Oh I,
why did I bury that letter in papers, a secret
that should have been said? Why didn't I guess
each drink of water was not for a dry throat's thirst but the spirit's

unstoppable thirsting for death. How long will my own guilt last? Shouldn't we want her back? Why did you send her back? All her best parts still twisted apart? Oh why?

# Decomposition

As if composed by Picasso being
cubist, I feel my single, simple solidarity
destroyed—every angle rearranged
and doubled, tripled, seen
from every side at once, on canvas it is art,
though somewhat frightening hung
inside the house, yet it is truly art, unless
you feel your body being slowly drawn
and quartered, torn from one self into several.
A woman with one eye. A woman weeping,
swallowing her tortured fingers. I can feel
her sorrow fully disarranged. Confused, as if
I too have limbs less solid than a brightly colored
paper doll, I cry, and not that only, more, there are
these pieces unidentifiable, like possibly that breast
so triangulated that it hurts. The rest are rearranged
or disremembered, pain infusing
every broken part. All his women are like that,
first, in life, a single form
then on canvas seething with a multiplicity
of parts or now and then, too few.

I feel myself this way, my being breaking up,
the limbs all disarranged, the mind
a loaf of bread already cut and waiting
to be served. How can one operate the phone like this

or just the hook and eye of something simple like a bra

when every finger's lost its hand, and all

the failing circuitry from head to hand is shot.

The legs you see in paint (Duchamps) again, again,

again upon a spiral stair. They've been divided

into many but are only two, this truth

they haven't learned and so can't walk. The grounds,

the spiral stair are lost to them; they're frozen

in their frame. But I am here, alive, to feel

my body pulled apart, my many artificial

legs in splinters. The rest of me, my single

eye, my arms are lost or misarranged, I feel

confusion like a shock of pain, the fever

or distortion for which there is no drug. Oh Winslow

Homer, dead I know, can you not come paint

me whole and happy like a child on a hill, a fisherman

midstream? Or please, just show me how to make

my body torn apart into a single, simple, solidarity of self.

# The Misapprehensions of Suicide

Is it harder to excoriate the skin with rasps and nails,

or harder to reject the mind's firm invitation

to scratch the forehead red? Oh easier

by far to separate the flesh from flesh

to see the blood lines leave their bloody

tracks. Should we go farther past the practicing

of blood and pain and more toward something

final, fresh, red blooms or wounds across the wrists?

There would be, of course, the mess, "the bloody mess,"

you say. The children forced to know you can destroy

yourself, their love, their care, tying pretty ribbons

in your hair, or patiently, painting every fingernail as well,

yet not enough to keep the big bad wolf at bay

if once you choose to open up that door.

## The Occupation of Desire

Even one eye can see enough to know

the world is full of things to want.

What do you want? A sled for Christmas?

a doll with plastic clothes? Or are you

not a child anymore but one who knows

to want to paint the kitchen green, a wooden bowl

of apples or of pears centered on the cedar table, or else

a garden of glowing roses, perhaps something more technologically

advanced a better car, a wider screen TV?

But if what you want is death, it's hard

to really want a vase of lilies, or the little pearl

earrings you saw downtown, or just the hint

of honeysuckle in the air. It is instead an effort

to want each day, each hour, each breath.

One feels oneself wanting a bridge, a knife,

a razor, whatever seems best that day, that day which is filled

with things I don't want anymore. Lucky I've never

wanted much except the unobtainable, peace of mind,

so there will be little to dispose of afterwards. Although sometimes

even now a book will cross my path that I feel

must belong to me. I bring it home and hope my family

will keep my library at least intact. If I could bring myself

to want more things, the perfect top, the perfect

watch, the perfect kiss, I could inch by inch draw

back from the precipice I've reached. Always

I remind myself I want my nieces to remember

their happy aunt who wanted to buy them

whatever they could want, or play whatever games

they fetch from closets and from toy chests. And they are

the one thing I want enough to keep my toes

just at the precipice, not even one inch over.

I should not be the one to introduce them to death's

desire for the living or when they're older to the madly misguided

ones like me who want to greet death by the work of their own hands

and enter into it ahead of their own time. I want

to leave their minds unbruised from this hard fact

at least for now and when it's learned I pray

it won't be me who teaches them this sorrow.

No matter how old they are, they are too young.

## Disembodied

Walking a half-block home takes time. I know
that not one thing has been removed; yet pressed
to doublecheck, I count the fresco angels gilded gold
and stoic on the cracked facade of the corner church.
They've never been restored. Instead
each body blooming breaks apart. Their faces
gouged and split, the cheekbones smashed half-
open, float completely disengaged but calm
like severed souls sustained, if not by faith,
then by an act of will, suspension
of despair. I find their fingers absent, chipped,
or shattered, and the hands, deprived of arms, keep
offering even beggars benediction. Lower to the left one sees
those giving up their hard-gained hell and hatred
loved like any leper's crutch, though useless
as the mutilated foot or rotted leg, the ones who've given up,
surrender to clamber a ladder that leans against nothing
but leads to an almost invisible city. A city where even amnesiacs
awaking whole and healed, again recall their name, their mother's
maiden name, and how, on newly bandaged feet,
to find their way back home through blackbirds'
bloody field or devil's den. They know their path,
like branches on the family tree, by heart; and though
it hurts to walk where streets are rock and rubble, broken
glass and twisted metal, still each solitary traveler trusts
their own last turning home remains untouched. Down here,

beside a wall of broken bodies breaking

into perfect parts, a bombed house burns, the landscape

falls apart, and even minds break down. Yet this

is what persists, a torso stripped of every limb

and sprouting one great wing, the willful force of life

that loves its injured head's good eye and partly

severed ear, as well as what's been lost, the splintered

jaw, a mouth, the torn-out tongue that tells you,

"Walk the half-block home. There's time

to find your own relinquished body

bleeding on the floor, to let the good hand's guilty fingers

tighten fast around the other gutted wrist's

well-opened vein, and pray." Does any prayer exist

for those who've found the sharpest edge, or made

the deepest cut but wish they had, just one more time,

refused to open all the doors and veins? They empty

to a ladder that leans against nothing, but look, it is rising

from my own damned blood and body. Having,

rung by rung, once started to abandon both,

I am afraid. I hear from far away, my lungs' compulsion

to continue breathing and my overflowing

pulse still swear

no bone or muscle will forgive me

my refusal to return; yet now it feels too late,

too hard to climb back down. An angel with no head

and half a halo tells me, "There is time and blood

still pounding in the heart to make one sound,

a call like some old jay's unpleasant caw,

cacophonous and sharp enough to bring some, one,

still living soul to pry the locked door open. "No!"

No one is allowed inside; though yet, perhaps, still

yes, some person not deterred by damage can come in, can find

their way across the warped and bleeding floor I've laid

between us. Not one perfect word is left to answer why,

but why should every broken, shattered, injured angel

on their wall, or faces followed on the street

seem all more whole than I? No voices

pounding nails behind their eyes says, "Die." But I

hear once and always carpenters all eager to apply the hammer,

lathe and saw to every thought until each one

cut fresh to fit the jigsawed frame says why—

if not one leaf unfurling, or rain creating mud

from dust, or beating heart, means more than crusts

the pigeons gather to consume, why not pick up

the hammer, saw, or nail, or find the window

left unlocked, the bridge, the stove, some sharpened edge

and leave yourself behind? Now when you've already

severed mind from pain—look up. You know the way,

like branches on the family tree, by heart. It isn't hard;

don't listen to the body, it wishes to go on with shoes

and showers, coffee, sweat, this grief like bandaged eyes,

insomnia, despair. Remember

that the body without blood can't feel; so why refuse

to let your feet go up the ladder you've prepared

yourself? And listen, listen—why call out

when only silence keeps your secret? I am sorry;

sorry for the bleeding arm, the blood

and words I've stolen out of silence, sorry

to have failed to die completely or correctly.

To have changed my mind, but still, forgive me, glad

one person with two whole, unbroken hands has come

to hold the ripped vein closed, to help me keep

what blood is left, unspilled, to hold

the tilting ladder straight until,

the way a late October aster lets its petals

loose, and looking dead, continues to survive, I can, myself once more

returned to me, continue walking home, amazed

that nothing more has been destroyed, disturbed, removed.

## Lakeland

One step down the hall to hell, I know I am condemned. Patients
pacing through the night to day are half delusional, not knowing
what they see does not exist except for their own eyes and therefore miss
what does, confused by what has happened and has not. Others
pricked and prodded by paranoia can't believe they are themselves,
for them the roommates and the nurses they see each day are not
who they appear but stone-cold killers, F.B.I., police and one time Condoleeza
Rice, and no one means them well but is about to listen to their
thoughts, to knife them in the back, to look them in the eye
and steal their soul. "Fuck You!" Screaming, shouting, hate
reverberate like violent twisters down the hall. "I rock you to painful.
I rock you to death," a woman shouts a hundred times or more
outside my door to someone only there inside her head,
but everybody hears and shouts out louder, reminded
by her litany of rage of their own unsettled angers. Chaos
whirls and dances, stumbles down the hall. Hostility stares out
of squinted eyes, accusing everyone of something bad. I've fallen
here against my will; my mind intact and oriented still times three
but locked inside somebody's cruel mistake, I'm trapped! A punishment for slicing up my skin to heal the fear I'd been abandoned
yet again with cuts I can control instead of loss I can't.
A choice no doctor chose to stop, although they saw it all;
they do not want to save me but only for their work to end without
dissent among the Doctors or the staff or my consent, to send me
far away where someone else's key locks out my only possible salvation,
love of those I love, because I've come to someplace where they give me

no more care beyond their work of knowing where I am, but never how

or why. It is a place one might reply that's just like hell, but only hell

can be like hell. This is not like it, but it is, and unlike purgatory,

maybe to be found on Unit Four or back where I've come from,

I've landed here where even God cannot arrange the moment of release.

# E.C.T. or Saving the Soul in Hell

The final roses reach full bloom. They're lustrous,

but not for me. I smell them and I know the smell

is sweet yet stripped of life's strong scent not even

some pale duplicate can reach my nose. For me the mind

has totally forgotten how to let itself enjoy a passing pleasure.

"Oh yes, no joy for you today, like everyday, from infinitesimally

small to large, the luster's gone." There is no warmth of want,

or of delight. The mind cannot accept, has not for months accepted,

even the simple fireflies' green light. So many things are drained

of pleasure that I hardly look about

at what goes by. It might, the world, be made of fog

with hazy landmarks to steer by. I know I'm breaking down.

The roses scentless blooms have told me I am lost.


But still I try to struggle on, unmoved by children walking dogs,

the sunset bleeding through the trees. I've grown as weak

as willow branches swaying by the stream. At every step I sway

and almost slip and yet I'm almost hard as stone; just once sit down

and I become almost too heavy to get up. Despair

begins to grasp my brain. Was I unhappy first? Well now I feel

unstoppable hysteria. To think about my life is worse, the sobs

cannot be quenched. Smiling is an art I've lost, nothing

makes it happen anymore. All the happy things are gone.

Each tightly shrouded by ashen, dusty sheets I can't unloose.

A never ending pain holds sway, lays out its noose each day.

I'm slowly filling up from some deep well inside with anguish
I cannot bear but do and as it spreads it slowly turns to stone.

Until at last, when I've become more stone than flesh
I can barely ride the bus to see my doctor because I can't
put on my clothes without three hours of hard work
or walk the ten long blocks without twice falling down or
weaving back and forth. After my last appointment, I must be
hoisted from the couch and heaved into my father's truck. The Doctor
tells me something I forget, but tells my father, "Take her
to a hospital before she lies back down and can't get up. She needs
electric shock," and I remember sitting in a crowded hall I hardly open
up my eyes to see, then being in a bed I almost can't get out
of on my own yet not once caring where I am.

Now I'm on a stretcher looking up at nurses looking down.
My special nurse is there so I am only half afraid as I could be.
It's strange, I want to die, but not by accident, unplanned by me.
Despite my partial fear unstilled, they're rolling me down
to the special floor with star lights overhead. The elevator holds
the whole long bed. We roll into a half-remembered room where all
the doctors crowd around watching the most important Doctor
spread cold jelly on my head. He's placing the things that hold electric lines
until I'm fully part of the machine, prepared to be electrified. I'm sure
there's proper terminology for that. Someone gently wraps
a cuff for blood pressure around my ankle and they pump it up so full
it hurts enough I think I have to scream out, "Stop!" but I swallow it
instead. The anesthesiologist means well. He smiles down

at me but I'm afraid of the mask around my nose and mouth. I'm scared
there won't be any air. There is but it is strange. Before I can decide
how strange all consciousness is lost. The doctors disappear to watch,

without me watching, the final exhibition of my cure, the quick
electrocution of my brain. When I awaken suddenly they say
it's over. Hardly any time has passed, The doctors have all
walked away, only the procedure was of interest. I feel the same
but hazy. Electricity running through my brain I thought would bring
me visions, something beautiful like Blake's; instead it bores a hole
through which events and thoughts and information, all quite random,
disappear. I do not feel their loss, but find some missing one by one,
when people tell me what I said and did or what has happened
in their lives and then I find just empty spaces
I cannot fill; although I might remember
what my friends retell, it's just a reminiscence of their reminiscence
not something I can see and feel; it's only worlds left dark. My journal
is as well a mystery to me except in spots. Though still not everything's a blank.

There's the catheter, embarrassing, but I remember that at the time
despite the fact I had to carry my urine with me in a jug until they deemed
it full enough again, I didn't care at all. Caring was too hard to do except
for one small thing, my smiling, happy doctor I care enough to want
to die if he should fail to come and even now I see him clear as day though
much of what he said has slipped through that damned hole. I remember he was wise,
but all the wisdom's lost. The patient's board declares that he's my Doctor
and everyday he comes but everyday I worry that he will not come, "Remember!"
he says, "Remember what I say." I never remember what he says, but this I do,
"You'll always see me unless my house burns down," and every time

he comes he chips away some little piece of all my anguish. He pockets it
to take away. No one else knows how to do this just the way he does.
I've trusted that he sees my soul and hopes to bring it back from hell.

Two times they've shocked my brain but still I cannot stand steadfast enough
or raise my arms above my head to wash myself. The nurses must wash me
in the special shower with the chair and hose. I don't care what nakedness
they see or fat. The nurses though are nice. They act as if it wasn't
too much work or ugly skin. They only say, "Now can you wash down there?"
And luckily I can, but how I look, what people see, is like a dream from another world.
It's not that I don't care, but care itself does not exist or how could I endure
this special job that can't be left undone yet can't be done by me. I can't begin
to care that all my visitors, or anybody else's, sees my mother feed me
with my plastic fork. I can't do it by myself. I'm only glad she's there.
It doesn't matter how it looks. I'm glad for visitors, I remember their faces
looming in my face. Some say we talked, but all I remember is their faces
looming up, and once my nieces came with their My Little Pony
memory game and somehow with my memory hole at work we played
until their time to leave arrived. I didn't win, not once.

The doctor of electricity and brains arrives to find me in the only chair
with arms big enough for me to get myself back up from (the big, pink
rocker I'm always glad to notice empty). He tells me how he wants
to give me another E.C.T. tomorrow and then another and maybe several more
than I can keep in mind. "Without that you're not getting better." I remember
that because I learned another thing I cared about. Getting better was something
I could want. After more electric shocks and visits from my happy doctor
the anguish slowly starts to melt. The hardest stone begins to turn to flesh,
the weakest limbs grow strong. Not only can I stand but I can get back up

*Terri Adamczyk* 43

from bed without the sidebars and all the strength I barely had at first.
When I am only flesh and blood not stone again and I am not a soul in hell,
but just depressed the Doctor says it's time to send me out. How strange.

The world looks like a foreign country, half familiar, half unknown.
Lovely yes, but strange. I miss my smaller world, its two hallways
and just two rooms I can go into, the public and the private one. It was
enough, but now I'm free to spend my time outside, or hold my mother's hand
all day and I will see my other kindly Doctor who sent me here before I fell
flat out apart. I'll show off all my newly made abilities, to raise my arms
above my head, to stand without the promise of imminent collapse, to talk
so clear a stranger even understands, to keep my eyes wide open, to pick
things up, to tell him I don't need three hours to get dressed, to tell him
what I do remember, to ask him how to keep from breaking down again,
for now that care comes back I care to keep my mind and body working
like they have before, but I'm afraid that this is just the answer he can't give.

I know my dread could come to life again, but I would care at least enough to send
myself and soul to shock once more despite the hole it bores inside my brain.
For now I'll fill that hole with what I've gotten back, my family no more
ushered out between the doors I can't go through, the calls to friends to tell
them I've been saved from hell at last. There are no roses left to smell,
but I'll accept the bare boned branches etched against the sky and outside air
that starts to hint of frost. I'll take my nieces' hands untangling my hair,
my sister who's massaging lotion on my feet. It feels like soft, warm,
summer mud that's soaking through my skin. The anguish may come back,
but I can hear my smiling happy doctor say one other thing I can remember
here, "There is only now," and I relax and let my sister squeeze my toes.

## Forgive Me (for the Doctor)

"Oh no" the reader, if I have a reader, says, "no more blood,
or rocks for self-predation, no wading into water
that can always steal your breath and energy, if you
go far enough beyond the breakers or allow
the rising tide to catch you up." No, no more of that—but why?

## II

This is what I see at night. I close my eyes
and death in different forms appears, better I should write
them word for word each one, than put the pencil
down and find the rope (I know exactly where it is) or knives
(how many can there be in just one room?). Forgive me
pounding out my pain like molten iron never cooled.
Forgive me, can't you, when whatever I can see becomes a why,

## III

a way to die? I say, "This is not my voice. It is the sickly,
sickening voice that worms itself inside the nerves." Its words
like waves inside a shell, can well be heard but don't exist.
Keep that shell pressed tight against your ear and hear my illness whisper,
"put down that shell and hear the real waves roll; they have their own odd
invitations to reject," but there is me, the one, the one
who walks along the shore, who, walking step by sickening step,
says no, no, no, not yet, no not, at least, today. The footprints
wash away, the words evaporate like mist, no sign of struggle

anywhere except inside my head, only pen and paper carry on

to say, "The wish to just be done with life is never done." I hear

hallucinations like a drowning ghost still trapped inside its shipwreck.

Me, the other me, finds cast along the shoreline

stones and seashells for which there is one word,

beauty. "Please, forgive me reader for so much

suicide and blood but think how often you have saved me,

catching up the worst true words and holding on. And others

writhing up from fevers coiled in the brain (as in, "Take out

an eye. The iron's hot. It's time to die.") You've twisted these apart

from words plucked off the tree of life like Madagascar jasper, Luna

Moth, a child's dripping painting, all in red. (You always

take my coat as well; where does that fit with one who plans

to die?) It's just the counterpoint I guess. You've caught my words

that spill from thoughts I hate to hands that work from word

to word alone, but caught by someone else's hands who know where mine

have been, my hands can almost bear to live as well as write. I need,

forgive me, reader, if you are a reader, please, I need you

like a lighthouse on the shore to steer me through,

through the drowning ghosts that sweat and shiver through

my mind. One light is all I need, or hands that hand me back

creation, ivy, peppermint, a mother giving birth, desires

to survive another day."

# II.
# The
# Amnesiac's
# Birthday

## A Surveyor's Guide to Departure

At dusk the lighted globe, ignited
by an aunt who's retired to a distant chair,
glows self-contained.
The equator cuts across eye level and South
America dangles before me suffused
with incandescent shades of palm and parrot
green. Spun secretly,
under soap-scrubbed palms,
illuminated continents revolve.

The windup clock, overhead, throbs
heavy as a fan revolves,
cleaving parlor voices into jigsaws
left unsolved. I'm submerged,
skinned knees sunk in the fabric
worn thin on the sofa, under yellowed piles
of China, Old Faithful, and Niagara Falls
swallowed whole by the stereoscope.
If I cross my eyes
the twin-divided, brown and yellow
depths of Yosemite merge,
like magic. No one remembers
it's after nine. I turn tiptoe
around the rag rug spiral.

At its border, consumed

by a rocker with swans' head handles,

mahogany necks clutched tight,

I rock, unseen

by the Audubon heron. Poised

over piles of Webster's

Unabridged, King James and Rand McNally, one leg

withdrawn from the marsh, it watches

a dragonfly unaware

of myself or the red clay continent

drifting under the cellar steps.

# Mile Marker

"Don't forget the mile marker
and you'll always know exactly where you were
when the car rolled off the road and parked beside the lake."
We all got out and mother, father told my sister and myself
how there had been a grownup growing out of love, enough to end the marriage
like an accident that wasn't a surprise. They saw it coming;
we did not. But, "Luckily," they said, "we'll all survive." Though something
in us dies for which there is no funeral, no sympathy, no mourning clothes,
no closing prayer. What makes us one, the family, has disappeared,
perhaps it drowned right there. It's true we're all alive
but we climbed back in that car not one but four, the ties
that bind unbound and how I wish I could go back
and hear the wind blow all those words away.

# The Amnesiac's Birthday

began when the world was no more than its shape and the language
of substance like cut flowers came without roots to the tongue. Violet first,
bloodwort, then crocus, quite simple concussions of sound rising thick in the throat
and repeated enough to be questions a doctor keeps asking, "What's wrong?
Is this all you remember?" Mimosa, magnolia, black walnut, walls
without windows, or only the thick, cursive script of the alphabet
twisted apart to print foxfire, fireweed, fat's
in the fire, forget-me-not, sweet everlasting,
last judgment, jack-in-the-pulpit? Like a surgeon
amputating rotten limbs, some angel in the head or heart,
has severed root from stem. The stump,
though nicely sutured, still feels like sin uncauterized,
its phantom twin on fire. "Hot, hot, hot." says baby,
patting fingers on that oven door. Hotter than hell,
apocalypse remains when words like criss-cross stitches
closing cuts have all been snipped and plucked away. Bandaged,
pink and puckered, stump and skin can't know
where all the broken parts begin; but say, like unstrung beads,
you saved them: stained glass, steeple, apple orchard, orchid,
thief. Each syllable, as if it were itself
the soul, appears to be alive and blooming, only
bloodless more like those decapitated swans you find
in public parks, or riddles I hear myself asked
yet can't answer, "Is this your house? Are these
your aunts, cousins, friends? Do you remember 1968,
Apollo, Tet, the bodies counted in their bags, a monk

on fire, maybe something later, simpler, like that president,

not quite contrite, surrendering his post to shame?" "No, no,"

you say you don't, because this is the sin

of omission forgetting not just who and when

but the sense and scent of forsythia, lily, myrtle,

mother. All amnesia's emptied cells are full of phantom

roots and limbs on fire. Who fuels the fire? Feel

the blisters bubbling in the emptied air. This is not

the garden where the world is named. Here

all names are flaming swords laid blade

against the skin. All night I write

gardenia, cosmos, red geranium; again, again,

again that bitter scent bleeds through. Lift back

the cotton gauze, the perfect print and there,

inside some stranger's bloody fist, or mine,

is what's been crushed, the petals, tangled

roots and strangled stem. Destroyed—

there is no anesthetic but amnesia; even amputation

leaves the severed limb as if it were a coal on fire,

burning. Not one lick of flame or crumbling ash is able

to slip back between the garden gates once locked. They are,

of course they are, chained shut against me. "But my mind,"

I am telling a salesclerk, who doesn't believe

it exists, "is just like that painting

you've never touched, all black with one red orchid's

throat, unstrangled, speckled, speechless, yet

too still." The hummingbird above should be sustained

by wings almost not visible; but see, each feather

is a clear, green flame, unburned. The pale, translucent petals, while storm clouds billow back behind them, should be

trembling. "Why does no leaf rattle or sound intrude?" Unless—

and this must be the truth—

it is no living plant or even dead. It is

a painting black and red, kept locked and motionless

inside a box. No scalpel sharp enough to bleed

bad blood from good, or hand, or breath of air can shake

or bruise it back to life. No. Because it is not now, and never was,

that red, no orange, though it is bleeding red, geranium

wrenched stem from pot. That was something living, maybe,

though don't say it, loved, and twisted grief to leaf,

quite dead. Yet there is now this oddly unprosthetic heart

still pounding through my head, "Your name, your name,

your name?" it asks as if that wasn't dead, as if

there were no punishment for shame, or church bells

casting out the broken, breaking pot shards, petals

damaged, damned, or blamed. Instead,

as unrelenting as the dark and light of every day

and every night, there is that ever running tide

inside the seed, the bulb, the brain, still asking,

"What is your name?" It asks and asks

again. Until, like grass from dirt, and word

from mouth, it blooms, not dead geranium, but

something that might be called nothing—or maybe this

tulip, peeling each clenched petal open, forcing

itself into blossom, remembering,

the water where even a stem without roots

might revive.

# Sanctuary

First there is the sanctuary, pulpit, pews
and up and down along each outer aisle are the stained
glass windows high and bright on days with sun.
Cream colored glass and wine red pieces, more like blood
when there is light, are curved and soldered into jigsawed
curves of emerald green, though mossy on a darker day.
These windows have no pictures only glass arched high enough
to let the sun stream in diluted by a bright
mosaic: cream, maroon and green. If I, not yet too old,
lost hold of what the service meant, I let my eyes
each week explore the different shades
of every color, watch the sun recede or brighten
just by looking at the red turn bloody.
Others might look down the rows of heads and think
of being baptized in the sanctuary turned from steady
wooden floor into a pool of water deep enough to plunge
the almost baptized under. I never got that far—
I picture being baptized by a rain of glass, the window
falling out and over me, my own blood added
to the colors on the floor. They are broken, splinter
sharp. Won't everyone here know I did this?
The minister is not at fault, so isn't it myself
who cracked the windows into pools of glass.
The minister will leave my mother and myself to pay
for sins I never understood. Not one tall window
really comes to fall on me, although it should. On walks

that must go past the Church, I feel the church bell,

not yet rung, insist I can't come in, and this is true,

the secret I don't know has put us out, how can I

come back in without some blood to pay for every sin.

Here and there where cracked cement holds bowls of sky

I see if I look right down, the bits of broken glass—

green for coca cola, amber for beer, and other nameless shards—

they tell me, "Take us home and we will show you days,

and months, and years, how long, how deep our cuts

can be." Now that window falls across me everyday

and leaves my arms as if they were

a stained glass window, only ugly, skin for glass

and blood like lines of soldered lead but red. Each arm

offers up a different view of injury and guilt

and every day another inquisition. Why?

But what if I should die without each unknown sin

accounted for and paid for with a penance

made of glass and skin. Now on walks that lead me past

the church I listen for the unrung bell to hear it call out,

"No, no more blood. We never asked for blood; the sins

of the father are not the child's." Should the child

see what the parents hide, does God provide

a host of tools for crushing out an eye as well

as glass and knives for making scars turned

white among the lines of glass cut skin? He does.

Yet when I touch the door there is no sound. I hear

nothing but the voice inside my head, but God's there too,

the handle blessed with absolution turns beneath my hand. It is

not locked against me. Inside I walk along the rows

of windows, touch each one, and nothing breaks. They are
silent whole and glowing. God doesn't ask me for my blood
or damage. The sanctuary floor has been removed,
its empty pool revealed without God's voice. I baptize now
myself, alone, in light and color and forgiveness, laying
bloody hands on trespassed skin, a promise not to break
the fragile surface of myself with sharpened glass I must
imagine God has not provided for my use.

## Ravished from our wishful eyes

our family (word by word like one strong current

rushing over rock) disintegrates in pain and fury, tears and cries.

So we who cherish stones stand beside bitter waters;

we cannot swim, but only watch with secret eyes

inside the scrub brush grown above the shore and looking down

from there our eyes believe they see

the rock that is our father, the stone

that is our mother, both engulfed by panic, passions, raging

with betrayal strong enough to drown or break

a husband, wife. The water here is deep enough to close

above our ears, and we are both too weak to dive down in

and gather up the ones we love, but even then

we disagree in silence over which is which

and tell ourselves our father, who we think

we see below, is really risen up and living on the other shore.

Not like a rock that one can stand on, steady,

but alive between the trees with sap like wine, the grass and fallen

leaves like tumbled beds; he lives a life not ground and shattered

but like a God, a Pan or Bacchus. Ask how many children

he might have, but we are his, right here

across the water where our mother's tears

are one more force to wash away

her face. By night we are afraid; there is no other day

when it is dark and leaves and branches, rabbits,

water rats make sounds like hunting men, or ghosts

in search of one who took their wives, but only we

are on this side, perhaps they plan to take us home,
to fill the absence in their beds. No. No.
We must stay here like lighthouse lights left out to call
our drowning mother back if she should ever be just light
enough to float (a dream we've made, a branch
might float but not a stone). Or could our father wander
close enough to see us here, to know
he is no Bacchus, only father ravished
from our eyes by dreams. He must wake up. Come home
to lift us up from sharp stones on the shore, to bind
our bloody feet, to heal our fears like thorns
and teeth. We can't escape alone. If only he might see
and cross our river flooded word by word and wound
by wound, could rise up from that pounding
water, not wishing to escape but save
our mother. We would be transformed like shattered rock,
not one, but for the moment, pieced together.

## Disappearances smaller even

than a fingernail pulled out or slammed
inside a door, are painful, burning purple, sloughing
off and growing tender. Before the nail grows back,
(a loss the body can absorb and then restore)
it hurts, though not the way it did the days, the months, the years

our mother fell inside herself
and disappeared as well; except for certain days she saw
our faces faintly far away and pulled herself outside
the deep, wet well to greet us, just as if she'd never left
her mind. She set us on the kitchen chairs, though not for lunch
but to repair our cuts and scratches, scrapes and splinters;
like a nurse she set the table with her tools,
her tweezers, Band-Aids, alcohol, peroxide, gauze,
mercurochrome. We've pried our own scabs off
to lure her here, though all she'd ever say, her cotton balls,
and gauze soaked stinging in the alcohol, was how
she missed us. Could we say the same?

Not with her words but with our blood
and wounds. Each time she came the long way back
is like a cancer in remission. Nothing lasts. Let her soft hands
tweeze a splinter stuck too deep to see. Just find
yourself relaxing, sure of that warm presence
brushing out our hair (the blond, the black) and watch, like happy

birthday flames blown out, her eyes

grow inattentive, blank, no matter we are children, hers,

she was unmoved and slipped away. We'd try

to call her back, but how? If we knew some way

besides our blood, we'd offer up our ears, our eyes.

Instead there's just this spiral path, this cord between

ourselves stretched taut across the crumbling well above

our distant mother's head. She's fallen farther down

without us. Just as gently as we'd combed her hair;

careful not to be too angry, or too selfish, we have prayed

"Forgive us our transgressions great enough

to take her from us." Why? Why leave our mother

lost in that dark well? For our father she rattles

the heavy rope (that creaks both up and down)

rattles it hard as if he'd save us. Utter the special prayer

or else unspeakable desire more than God's to save,

if not ourselves, our mother. What if God delivers

only one and we, more two than one, are left

to look far down

the uncapped well where we might see the glitter

of her eyes or tears, perhaps. It's hard to love

a glimmer or a God who will not give our most beloved

back her mind completely healed, the wish to be restored. No.

This God picks just the other one with better

greater things to do than carry children

back to bed; he, that other one born fast and forceful

who doesn't love us first but second, maybe third of all

the women he's allowed to love. Still we loved them

better, mother, father, than ourselves. As marked and guilty

as we are, we could not find, or see, or go where we are

loved despite the red and oozing lines across our skins,


the shapes of sin

like hieroglyphics. If we only knew exactly what they said

they might call forth our mother from her absence.

What happens if you look too long, too deep

for those you miss like amputated toes and feet; you fall

too far for being saved—just the one who loves us best

is here already fractured, incomplete and blind. She cannot

see us now or drag us out; although, she mumbles

"Oh I love you." We would pray we'd not offended

God with sins we know we have like splinters stuck

too deep to see and haven't found in time. They leave us

rotted, rotting, spoiled, young.


We're nothing anybody wants to salvage. Though there remains

a faint existence we can hear like spiders

moaning in their webs. That voice (some God

we can't be sure is ours) has sworn in echoes

circling stone to brackish water, sworn. It is allowed

to cry for help if one is waiting for the world's

cut grass and wild trees of life that can forget

their death and love the rainbow

and the stones, the dirt and sand, the turtle

in one's sisters' hand, so small it can be saved

and taken from the sand to sea. Aren't we

small enough for hands to lift us free; or only small enough

for predatory birds to peck and prey, and then

one is allowed to cry and can.

## Please God Unmake Me

or at least speak more softly in my ears, or
finish offering me knives and glass, forgotten
nails to take away an eye or two, who knew
when one was small and playing kickball
on the lawn, that badness day by day
was welling up inside? Lying flat upon my back
to see the sky, I feel the gnawing punishment of guilt
inside and know it is too late already to be good
enough for God or even grownups. Inside my throat
there is a frozen lump; it aches with fear
that people day by day can see God's sentence
written not just on my heart
but on my skin. "There is no heaven for yourself,"
God whispers, "only life and life to suffer through."
Because it's true, the sins of the child are written
on the arms and eyes; their hands write messages
from God with glass. I've fallen farther than my parents.
Just take out my eyes that see them, father, mother,
empty out their wedding vows
(in sickness and health) upon my lap like lacework
to repair but being close to blind, I've failed
to fix my mother and my father having tossed
his vows aside is light and leaps away. I am
sinking with the weight of sins he has disowned. Why
should God rain all of them on me? He's saying, leave
a mark for each, a bruise, a cut, a fractured

bone and I'll remember sacrifice as well as sin.

The father's sins should not be all

there is to life. But if I must be forced to hold

so many sins like stones, so close, please unmake me

starting with a different string that like a firmly knotted net

cast out will hold the passing beauty

of the minutes not the sins

of those I love.

## And still I am waiting

for what seems simple to become
contented, happy, glad that I am floating
in this small river where my hair drifts out
around me, fish brush past, my arms
are strong enough to pull me
to the center where a current gently tugs me,
hair and arms and legs, downstream.
I should be happy, if I stopped to look
through water clear enough to see the rocks
below and fish dart by. My feet just brush
the smooth, bright stones, my fingers barely
touch the scales of fish escaping. I should be
contented, glad to be. Instead I just enumerate
the happiness I could feel if only I remembered how
—if pleasure were not locked (for years, for months)
away and buried in my brain
which feels not life and water
buoying me up, but solitude enough to keep
my body sealed and separate. This is too small
a place to drown, too pretty, trees and boulders
children might arrive to climb and find me
lifeless. Even still not drowned,
not dead, my death is filled with guilt at leaving
just a mottled corpse for someone else to grapple
on to shore. So I am waiting, hoping still to outlast
my urgent pleas to die by picking out the brightest

rounded, smoothest rock to find the key

to open up the box and feel, not wretched reeling

to be living still, but the beauty of the stones

I've gathered up on shore against the day my joy

arrives and I can touch their beauty

without a thought of hitting each one hard

against my head to crack the lock and burst

the box ajar, and then the gentle water

keeping me afloat will lift my hair, myself

in simple journey far enough downstream to feel

no urge for death enveloping my body and my mind.

No wish for reaching down to currents deeper,

stronger than my arms, but life and strange contentment

spreading (finally) through my skin and crackling

through each nerve. They spare me

breath by beggard breath, and stone by stone, from drowning

or from breaking much too much to fix. For what?

Please, not some other dark, unvarnished time,

but for the white and mottled pink stones

smooth beneath my palms, the breadths

of green lit trees like spires overhead

or sudden boulders flat and warm below my back

like miracles, their solid substance, just for now,

sustains. I hold those rocks I carried out

to shore (some weight inside my hands to pin

me back to land, this boulder buoying me up

to life). I feel each stone I've saved worn smooth

from agitation. Their colors gray but scored with white

like frozen lightning or a brain wave

stopped and studied, others

speckled black and white as if

some fireworks exploded into stones

like sky but pink, the white ones small and pocked

with holes like someone's face, the eyes, the nose

and mouth. I should be sad to leave my death behind

but feel the joy of feeling given back

to me without more years or months of waiting

for a truce that lets me save myself

with just a few bright rocks to prove one can go down

into the river and return with one's right mind.

# Rites of Inflection Downriver

Though I bandage both ears with my hands
I am always the minister's daughter. I hear
echoes that swallow my tongue. They persist.
Since you left, I have not returned
to the poise you brought up
in the dark-grained pews. But uprooted

among the pines and the birches'
white gestures, the Doxology lingers.
Its offering hums back
over tire-rolled ruts, red dirt,
I've paced to the river's bend. Remote
from the gathered rumbling, I cannot deny
how the vibrant notes seeped
from my hands. I have left

what you left and did not intend
to remember massed voices
wading toward invocation. Here
the Meherrin surges. Your own voice keeps rippling
like Joseph's narrating dreams or Jonah's
raised in a fish belly, rattling
with cadences not yet submerged. But it isn't
the words that I hear. These days

my hands flick the water. Snapping

cedar-gold showers, the tips of the fingers
fidget. Your sermons are stored
in the cellar. Their scriptures
I cannot remember as clear as the hair, flattened
strands, clenched around each wet face you withdrew
from the waist-high pool. What persists,

while I perch on the root-webbed ledge
of this river, are feet, scuffling
heels, meeting floorboards to rise, and the raw-
shaven throats of the choir. Their resonance
taut like your own, preaching fisherman, fleshing
the fish and the loaves, calling out, "John
the original Baptist," before you moved on.
I could not go back. With both feet

pressed to this riverbed, wading, the water
that washes my ankles is water. But drawn
through its current I find
my hands have retrieved
their composure; entwined while the simplest
inflections stir in the ear's canal.

# Spring

Hyacinth, Iris, Azalea—beautiful,

beautiful stasis, purple, pink, ivory flower and bush,

but everywhere dandelions not stopped by garden

rows or borders have gone to seed quickly and each one

ready to fly, only first make a wish, but a wish

is no simple thing, close your eyes and blow

off every seed. It's not so easy to accomplish.

A total seeding

like a wind creates, is what one's breath

must be; so strong and steady that it leaves

the crown completely bare. Now wish.

But this is just a wish; it may not grant

one's greatest wish, so wish

for common, necessary things, not quite impossible;

one might wish to catch a black snake with one hand

or see the lunar eclipse burning itself, blood

red, and all around me yellow flower-weeds

take greater root and seedlings having flown descend

to settle farther down below the grass and dirt.

It's spring. It is enough.

# III.
# The Angel
# of Hoarding

# There is no simple way

to wage one's war against this stark, malignant
sleeplessness. One might lie down and feel
the pillows sink beneath one's head, yet still no comfort
comes. Just fear's resharpened blade pressing lightly
across the chest; the choking hands at rest around
the neck. No sleep can be allowed to lay its gentle fingers
on the eyelids, yet it whispers
in one ear as if a lover lay there softly saying
like a lullaby, "Oh sleep. Sleep. Listen, let the restless
hidden eye give in and close. Lie down." I feel
sleep's first beginnings smoothing out my hair, the eye
inside draws open wide, can feel the danger
of succumbing to a sleep that isn't sleep but breathlessness
and death. Who can save the body when every eye
is closed? The stomach writhes like roots
are taking hold. Each breath needs all my effort
to avoid the greater struggle growing in my lungs
where a black, asthmatic flower blooms, its sticky,
heavy petals rising in the throat. By sitting up
some subtle shift of leaves allows a salt spoon's worth
of air to trickle through the lungs. But this
is insufficient to remain myself. I see these shaking hands
slough off to be replaced by someone else's.
If only they might bleed, I'd know that they were mine.

My legs, as if they too belonged to someone else,
keep twitching, tremors forcing me to give up getting

out of bed. And now those gentle fingers

soothing me to sleep have pressed

their thumbs around my throat. The flowers blackened

crown creates a lump for them to press against.

Its roots call out for water and my mouth is left too dry to call

for help. My mind, a spinning wheel,

says: "You're not yourself;

you're almost dead, bled dry from every cut it takes

to know you are yourself. You aren't. Your self will not

come back." This self, whatever's left of me,

is looking at its unfamiliar fingers, knows they are

the lover's stronger hands which plan to squeeze

my throat completely shut, the moment

I have closed my eyes, although, the restless eye

inside says, "Don't sleep." If I don't sleep

I will hear the spinning voices tell me

more and more how hard it is to breathe. "Lie down.

Sit up." Why am I not myself despite these lines of blood

that must be mine? The brutal lover saying, "Sleep,"

is not a friend but fraud who whispers not just "Sleep,"

but also, "Die." It wants my body for itself

since that self suffers too and would destroy the pain of being

while I sleep. I will not sleep, won't shut

that inner eye, won't let the hands still trembling in my lap

begin to crush the flower, and its roots, and something

like a squid's beak tearing through my stomach. Why not

destroy brain and body both? Because they are myself

each night creating pain to crush the wish for sleep.

I'm forced to feel the sluggish turning of the hours

splitting my skull in two. That one who cuts

can whisper, "Sleep, sleep, sleep." Yet I cannot bear

the weight of pain and unstopped wakefulness. But look

it is no other self but mine who is my own oppressor,

who must find the aching, bleeding path to stand the push

and pull of sleep and death thrust hard against my

spinning mind, of course that must be stopped. Instead

of giving in to midnight's plea for self-obliteration

from which no light or life can come, allow myself

to feel sleep's fingers, to smooth

the bruised skin underneath the eyes, so the split

skull knits itself together; the inner eye prunes back

the choking roots and leaves, the buds in flower throughout

my lungs; at last that one calmed eye stands guard

while uncontaminated sleep takes hold.

## Occupant

"This is the room," I might say
like the landlord whose family reminds me
this isn't my home. On the opposite side
of their door I must hear the sharp
sound of their son as he pounds
the piano, staccato. Staccato
comes through, but it's only the coda
my fingers play
tapping, like moths against glass.
If I cover my ears
I see each window offer a serial view of the roof. For myself
there is always the weather vane,
shaped like a rooster, set
swiveling. Its beak bites the fist
of the wind. When it dies I am looking
for hands like my father's to open
this window. As if I were always
the child he chose to forget, I remember
he leaves, or he's left. Going deaf,

I resist but the question is why
should the maples keep lining the gutter
with leaves? They turn black and the gray shingles
plunge into evergreen limbs, where I've never seen
even a sparrow. Not me, but the child
still facing the weather's tough beak,

like a stoic my parents have raised

by mistake, is reminded by even this sunset

of standing, as if it were safe,

with a mother and father beside me;

our feet in the shallowest edge of Ontario.

All we can see through a screen of thick pines

is the light, like blurred ink. Then my mother says,

"Look at the sun," and my father goes hunting

for stones on the shore. I am left

with the sixty watt bulb of a room I would rather

desert, heat and light growing hard

to maintain. Even now it is cold


under quilts where my weak eye takes root. It sinks

back through the patchwork of yellow

and plaid, salvaged cloth, to an acre

of golden rod; flannel and cotton

grow weeds. When they bloom I am wrapped

in the heart of an empty lot grown wild where even

the one who won't hear must keep seeing

her mother's smooth hands planting

irises. Tugging flowers

from flannel, her child forgets

she is lost and lets patches

of pine barrens cover me. Nothing

but trees and a lake. I wade back to a beach

where the pine trees take hold, and my father lets go

of my hand. I go deaf. When he leaves

without looking for stones or me, I am sinking

my hands below water an inch

at a time. Because cedar bark darkens

this body of water, my fingers turn rust

to the wrist. He has left me

a mother, who isn't his wife after dark, whispering

"Look at the sun," but it sets,

and before it is over

I want to go back. In the pattern of plaid

I find fistfuls of pine needles, nothing but dried

marrow crushed by my thumb. It is cloth

I am holding against me. And pounding


up hardwood steps, the landlord leads

his boy to bed. To the tune of Dvorak's

"New World" he is singing a song about whales

in the deep blue sea. Footsteps mount stairs

like a metronome. Three kinds of love

on the landing; "Where are you?" "Sleep tight,"

and "Don't go." Find their way

past the door I have closed. To go out

I must step

through the frame of their family

without one. It's better

to sleep. When I dream it's the rooster

or maybe the wind, scratching open

the marrow of pine—I can smell

its strong pitch—summer sap that reminds me

of something I've lost; holding tight

to the evergreen arms, it's myself

not the child who speaks.

## If I could write

right now, I'd know
my hands had been unbound, left free
by years of gnawing at their knotted ropes.
These hands are free but have forgotten how to be
themselves. There is a white-hot surge of blood
let loose, more than pins and needles, more
like heated tar or lava burning from each wrist
to tip—a scalding from within, but slowly,
slowly the blood burns less and all the ligaments
and muscles whisper, "Who are we to you? We've been
so long removed from life; although, we're grateful
to your patient, worn-down teeth. And are amazed
they've always known; it seems, their purpose, how
to chew the stale or moldy bread served once a day,
and how to chew our ropes away, and we, so white
and flapping like a bird's wings though we cannot fly,
but try and try to know our purpose. Even you
to whom we're reattached don't know us really—we seem
strange to you, too small, too big, too lifeless. Last you'd seen us
loose we were strong and brown, could break a branch
and snap it into two, could gently cup a baby's head
in just one hand, could push a child on a swing. But these,
these things here, just so newly reappeared have yet to hear
the nerves that sing and sew these apparitions on my lap
to life. They're white and weak, the fingers tremble,
as we speak, like worms that have a purpose of their own. Perhaps

we wish to be rebound, perhaps that is exactly

what we have become, two appendages

tied tight again, so all choices disappear. It might have been

against our will at first, the fingers needing to be free

to pull up weeds, to pick tomatoes, to put one's hand inside

another's, both necessary if we wish to brush our hair or climb

above this wall that has been built around us. Is outside worse

than where we are? We cannot know without the hands."

The body says, "You must remember who you are

to climb the wall to set us free. Don't let each finger

think, but be." They're trembling still but I know

they are my own hands. Not yet strong but free

to pull us stone by stone from self-composed captivity.

# The Presumption of loss

Desertion, Death, Cholera, Whooping Cough, Small Pox,
Consumption. How many babies died? How many Indians' lives
are swallowed up into the earth after our ancestors offered them
blankets to warm themselves with small pox and wool, and we
ourselves, our bodies are totems of death
and disease, the only cure, immunity,
and a powerful will to live. How many open
their eyes alive? Blackfeet, Mandan Clans
disappearing in only one season. How many more people leave?
Is that right how people just leave, take the wagon train west
and leave their neighbors, Dear Sister, a brother afraid
to risk all on the Oregon Trail, or worse the ones leaving
safety to follow an ill-advised path that sounded much shorter
but only grew longer and longer until most all of the oxen
and cattle have died, belongings discarded on either side
(lightening the load), "Little girl shouldn't you put down
that doll?" And she never did. Its small face a refuge
from death. At last in extremis, trapped
by a truly impassable pass, they are stopped as the snow fell
fast, the ones who survive their bodies' continued collapse
go on by taking flesh from their family and friends,
goaded by their seemingly faithful companion,
starvation, which whittles away taboo that is dead under
frozen snow. To live here one cannot bury the dead, too hard,
and they might be needed. One must give credit
where due: at least, they waited for all spirits to have taken

leave of their hardened, hunger-wracked bodies, before

anyone guilty but hungry, consumed what they could of the dead.

Not the Lord's Supper, of course, blasphemous really,

but useful, perhaps. Suppose they had never left,

wouldn't they still be alive?

## II

But some other ill-fated voyage would go on instead,

that ship that was trapped

in the pack ice—trying, trying to find the way

through the polar sea—they failed.

But nobody died, except for the sled dogs the sailors loved;

only slowly the growing idea

that there weren't enough seal, enough penguins, enough food

for men and dogs both, they swallowed their tears

as they ate. Though all of them might have died

without their dogs, and if somebody couldn't pull out a gun

and dry-eyed shoot them with one shot, humanely in private. It took

two years to cross over the polar ice. Nobody cried

except that once for the dogs, but they cheered

when the opening ice became the open sea,

wild clamoring, pounding their leaky boats. Strong arms

almost too leaden to row. Hard choices. The weakest

can hardly bail. At the first approachable freckle

of land, an eyebrow of rocks not sand, an unassailable cliff

overhead, the captain is already choosing who

with their bodies failing too fast, must disembark, their lifeboats

pulled up for some cover. How can they not cry when he leaves?

But they believe, as believers do, he will bring them home.

# III

Those stronger struggling, reeling against heart-crushing
water like cliffs falling over them, filled almost to sinking
the bailed boats rise up enough to go on until they are carried
at last to their initial point of departure. A barely crossable
island if forced to land on the good side.
They had to land on the glacier side,
determined to push their way through to find
on the other shore, the only indigenous people,
whalers, amazed a dead captain had reached them
alive, like Rip Van Winkle arriving
from another time. The whalers who had thought
he had died in the ice, (The Endurance and all hands
lost), had to lay hands on them all to believe
they had truly survived. Offered a true ship,
the captain pushed back through the waves of presumable loss
each hour fearing ice had already surrounded
his men, crushing their flickering lives, having already swallowed
their refuge. Instead they were living still, suffering starvation
and dreaming of crème brûlée, pot roast, tea and toast, fish
and chips, all the while living on limpets and hope. Everyone
lived. Only later, at home, did they find themselves
fraught with the guilt of survival. How many men went
to the Front? Who emerged from the Polar dark
as if they had lost all their luck and died in the gas
and mud more deadly than Polar ice?

# IV

Whoever survived bullets and bombs and flu
saw families and friends consumed by an influenza
nobody understood except for its ending, most often death.
Each death survived leads to another possible death to try
one's soul against, and if you don't die then,
surely you end up breathless, breathless with polio crippling
the hot summer months. Lucky you've lived on
in an iron lung, the body's death hidden away
inside a mechanical capsule, half casket. "Keep
you chin up," the nurses say, "at least you're alive."
But unless the orderlies wheel you down the long
linoleum hall, you can't leave. Your visitors
dwindle, young men, family men, friends signing their names
and swearing to die in the army, navy, air force, if not

shot quickly by bullets then slowly by tuberculosis.
You can't leave your cure in the sanitarium,
unless you cough up your death or throw
yourself into survival, cured by fresh air and good luck,
so then you can desert those still infected.
Right now you're forced, (before the cough) to live,
we're forced to live with the space in our lives
where those who have passed away from us had lived
some with their habits of rocking out late on the porch,
or drinking hot coffee on days so sweaty everyone
has a slice of wet watermelon. Their pictures

will soon disappear from the carefully chronicled
lives in the black-papered album. Later
other familiar faces have flickered out as well. But some
had a longer time to sit with the bride on the porch swing,
not planning to leave each other's side
for a long time yet, and their luck holds out.

# Do not see but believe

the bombs like burning earthquakes shaken from the sky

are deafening, smoke and cries. They rise,

those sounds, from devastated worlds (is any country

not a world?) to which, Thank God

we were not born, or those from which we've fled

so long ago we hope we will be saved from mourning

sons or daughters at the school a few imploded blocks

beyond the embassy; yet still we mourn

the counted and uncounted dead we would have known

if we had not survived the crushing

crowds, the terror, to emerge

beside the final chopper's ladder just within

our grasp, one minute left to lift the last few free

of bombs and bullets, bloodied bodies

on the streets. Do not see but believe

those left behind will not be left with lives

they used to have but with a life like lead

in someone else's hand; our neighbors scrambling

back through old debris to what remains

of what they own, a broken, twisted home blown

down inside a hole still burning, besides the babies

in their arms, the sons and daughters small enough

to sling across their backs, they know they only own

themselves and later less than that. We are

too high above their pain to know its size and shape,

and shame of being captured in another's hand. We feel

our shames' less deadly form of leaving all our neighbors,
cousins, teachers, others' children glimpsed like poppy blossoms
on the street all beautiful but bloody. Why will we
survive although transformed from citizens
to refugees? We are flying to embrace
our immigration to that other world where order
often smothers chaos, where snipers have not spent
their days on one high hill preparing people
for their place within his random range and

rage. It's clear from bodies scattered right out there
along the necessary path for water and for bread
that thirst and hunger can be ended by a stranger's
bullet in the heart or head. We who do not see him
know he's there; those thin red hairs have sighted,
sifted everybody in their path until there is
that final second to decide who lives, who dies. The sniper
who we cannot see, but know to be persistent
or enraged, perhaps deranged, or callous and indifferent,
bored by death or maybe more by life. Which one
it is we cannot know, but only know
he's there, so only those most desperate
send their children to the fountain's spout. We,
ourselves, have cheated death by leaving, living where there are
no bombs, no ground like Krakatoa
burning not by force of nature but by force
of living hands with plans and planes, or only
unhealed anger burning in the walking soldier's bones.
We cannot believe unless we see it, chaos

in our own yards, here, like worlds and worlds,

destroyed and built again, we cannot believe

what can't be seen that those still living

can be given back a life lived by its own volition.

Do not believe but know it will be hard. Hard

to free the prisoners weeping in another's fist

clenched tight and forced to write

the blasphemy of what is not believed but done;

there will be those who learn to kill, not only men

but boys, there will be those they've killed not soldiers,

more like families on the road, everywhere there will be

someone to be saved as well as those who've lost whatever blood

they needed to survive this conflagration where compassion

is just the rules of war or likely less. It will be hard to hear


the thousandth terror of the billionth or the sixteenth

orphan who knows a world of limbs blown off, the city

where each day there will be less and less of more and

more, less water, fewer tents, less food and fewer names,

(one's own included) to remember. They have never seen, but everyone

believes that story where parents, worn

and muddied have arrived at last inside

the world of orphans and searching, find their nameless

children, hungry, thirsty for their mothers

and their fathers who like magic will have saved

their lives; let them, reassembled, be their own small world

among themselves, the floating island of the father,

mother, sisters, brother; all believe their lives,

if not their limbs, will be restored this way.

## Gauguin Paints The Mother, Praise, "Ia Orana Maria"

The child rides on her shoulder, resting
his cheek on the crown of her head. She ballasts
his weight with her own hands' strong fingers spread
like a bird's wings over his ankle. Others
are gathered behind them, three women, one
is an angel whose face is protected by flowering
branches, and farther, behind them: volcanic
blue slopes, vegetation, a village surrounded
by palm trees the color of shadow and shaped
like a body that's already learned to be bent
without breaking. Right now, the woman are looking
away from the water that's ready to carry them
all into baptism. Standing in perfect proportion
to intimate mountains, worn smooth, and the ground
that supports them, each body is solid and steady,
so calm you'd refuse to believe they're expecting
the one worst thing that will happen.

But not at this moment, when even Gauguin
could have carried the child as well as its mother
away from whatever is rising above them
to high ground, quite blue in the distance; but shelter
this distant can't shelter; he's painting,
instead, the soft substance and steadying weight of their hands:
two women's folded with reverence, another's

still holding her son's foot against her, his own hand

at rest on her shoulder. Their faces are perfectly quiet,

completely alive, like the delicate shells

of each body unveiled by a tidal wave lifting itself

to completion. There's only a moment

to gather one's breath, to look back

from the terrible thing that is coming, to capture

the perfect proportion of grace before grief.

## Praise God

who lets perhaps these blessings flow right here,

right now; the sunset breeze is no asthmatic

cough or numbing blast to fight against tonight—

it's barely cool, a tickling breath that turns

one's thoughts away from hurricane force winds like danger,

anguish, drowning, immolation, grief, from when and where

such storms accumulating strength at sea might strike,

to how these clouds, no longer white,

are mottled orange, how beyond the railroad tracks

the trees become one black and solid mass, unbroken

though the air that lifts each little hair from hand to head,

transforms what can't be seen, the light-extinguished

leaves, to living tongues. They make a sound

I hear like voices through a wall. A bouncing ball and children's


game cries thump and echo through this field still green-

gold where last light turns their soft blades

bright as sheets of water rippling out

in darkening rings around me, not becalmed,

but moored in a heartbeat's pulse of praise: Thank God

that this one day is ending softly, kindly,

all my family coming home for potluck grace

and love are well. Thank God—don't think

how long before that glistening ripple widens

from the center to the shore, or what could happen

in the night. If I could think of nothing more

than what's below my feet, this grass, this green,

this lake, I might believe all's well

enough to not just count but taste each breath,

each blessing, every blazing blade of light.

## Incomplete Frescoes

The walls were thick plaster. Overhead

one bulb, just lit, stretched shadow box

frescoes across the room's rough sides. A metal bedstead,

a woolen blanket, even in August

the mountains were cold by dusk.

Standing at the chesma

where plastic water jugs are filled,

I shiver in the cool air sinking

closer to the Prizren Valley. It is simpler

inside the room. Its oak door

shuts out the hallway and soft-step

passage of old people

climbing the outdoor steps to bed.

Only a donkey's bray intrudes

through the window, two stories over the footpath.

And only, from the other bed (her thin face

pressed between blanket and wall), my Marxist friend

cries because I still believe,

like the peasants found in the frescoes

of the valley, fading into plaster walls.

# The Angel of Hoarding

has opened the door I keep closed to show you the paths
through the place that belongs more to what I have kept
than to me. There's so much that even I can hardly inhabit
the rooms, though of course I've made aisles to get
to the bed, and the stove, and the bathtub. No one has ever
come in but the angel of hoarding has offered this tour to let
me feel, through somebody else's clear eyes, how it keeps me
surrounded by paper and hidden from people I cannot ask in
to see how even my bed full of books doesn't welcome me, nor
does the chair full of clothes. Let me show you how simply
it starts with emotions for things you can fill in for people. First

there's this rock a good friend who lives far away
has chosen to send to me because she's aware
I love rocks but not how little room I have for one more.
This lump of dried clay, my nephew made when he was three.
You can't tell what it is but I know that he made it
for me. And I have to keep it forever because now he's grown up
and will never make such a strange thing again. I need this
to know I was once the aunt he sometimes forgot and called
mommy. Even better he came into the house and using his three
year old eyes never saw anything strange in the towering
papers, tables cleared only for one, clothes hung over the chairs,
envelopes everywhere. I miss that small boy. How
can I throw this away when it tells me he loved me so much?

Look here at these miniature bottles of scented oils I keep meaning
to use, but I don't. My father sold them and these were left over
when they finally stopped selling. They cannot be thrown
away because they're still good. It's been at least ten years
that I've saved them, but if the time finally comes to put them
to use and they're gone I'll be sorry I tossed them away. These
are the papers my mother brought home every day. They are
containers of monumental events and nostalgia if ever you pick
out an old one, you're reminded again how things were, where
you were, what you wore when the space shuttle exploded, or
John Lennon died. These are the magazines I didn't get a chance
to read but should, I can't throw them out till I do. Then here

is a jar full of shells I collected along the shore on days
I was brought by my parents to stand at the edge of the earth.
Here are the letters my friends have sent long ago or just now.
They are full of sentiment I'm loathe to discard though it's rare
that I read them again, but the first time I read them I know
that they have to be mine forever; unless it's a card with only
a signature, that I can toss, but what if the card itself is uniquely
beautiful? That is a quandary. I have boxes of letters, piles
of books I have read or am meaning to read. Any book that is
a great work of art or pierced my heart like a spear I must keep.
I have notebooks of all of the children's art work. Any squiggle
they made I must keep. Beside them are all of the papers
marked saved, but not even neatly stacked and capped by a sloping
tower of magazines. I have legal pads everywhere covered with my own
cryptic script. They are my life written down. What can I do but collect
them, although there are more than can fit in any one box? They're all

out of order, undated. No way to work my way back to their origins,

but they are full of my poems and dreams and distress and great joy

I might well forget if they weren't written down. Memory is malleable; words

last as long as the paper's allowed to exist and the mice don't make nests

of them. Papers, papers with words, my own, the children's, my parents'

are treasures to keep. And then there are things that have been beloved.


How can I throw away the girls' favorite animals, trolls, or their marbles,

all sizes, all colors? I have all the things that they gave their hearts to

with full force. And things that they might want to use like a packet of pipe

cleaners, carpet samples, four kinds of glue, two with glitter, piles of felt,

play dough supplies, spools of thread, or just spools and yarn in as many

colors as possible, although I knit poorly, if ever at all, but it all could be

used, if not by me, then the children. I still have the jacks from when


I was eight although now I've grown old. I remember how many things

disappeared in my mother's own chaos, how it swallowed my toys and my joy

so fully that now I'm afraid to let go of even the clothes that don't fit (I pray

to lose weight), or even the things that are broken like the Mexican clay

angel whose arms have fallen off bit by bit, her cupped hands at the wrist

going first, the rest of them lost from being unsteadily perched

on a pile of letters meant to be filed because I imagine they're all

still important. Some people, like my sister, are sure to ask why I have kept her.


But can anyone ever throw an angel away, even in parts? In museums

they keep all the bits and pieces of whatever survives the long past. I love her.

Doesn't it say to me what I believe in, that I have a dark angel,

but one with no arms to reach out and save me when I'm locked

on the psych ward trying hard to believe I am sane, or when I'm so sad

I can't cry any tears? They were all in her beautiful hands
that I saved but then lost in the chaos around me. It's true
that if I just throw things away I might find those cupped hands
still holding my tears and could at last cry for my jumbled up,
bittersweet life, but perhaps I'd lose things more important

than tears, like my heart on each page of my journals, or
my carefully doled out remembrance of happy days held
in a small child's passionate art that reminds me of watching her paint
while she sang a small song about five little ducks and a frog
and I was so glad to be the safe gate in her world
holding back monsters, bad dreams and terror. If I threw
it away, where would the happiness go? How would it come
to my mind? How would I know I exist without
letters from friends who believe I belong in the world
and my tenuous equilibrium might have been
hiding in something I tipped in the trash? I never believed

what I know you would say, "All of them live within you," but
since I am nothing, then how can that be? And with or without
her simply crafted but broken black arms and cupped hands at least
I believe an angel can watch me and share my confusion, my pain,
my depression that holds me in bed, unable to open the door
because no one can see how I live. Only my angel looks on
without judgment and loves me, but I must remember how much
I believed my dark angel was there when my body caved in
to depression and they whisked me away to the psych ward
without her. Her broken body is only a shell, a reminder
of what I believe, that there's always an angel beside me

to sit there through all my long hours of pain and maybe

the real one's still holding my tears, waiting and waiting

for me to remember we are not in our things but ourselves.

# IV.
# Embracing the Orange Hour

## Locked inside

the borders of a closed estate, there are,

there always will be, artists not allowed

to paint, not even half an orange,

rinds placed neatly on a chipped, blue plate

to prove it is an orange eaten

and uneaten both; a black sky overhead filled,

not with stars, but grey-brown iron bars—they are

the cell that plunges down around the painting

as if it were both key and door, the artist key,

the painting door; but here the jailer is the key

and door that opens in, not out, (the border

crossing of a smaller state). Next door

the startled playwright written into prison, word

by word continues, not with paper or a pen,

but with an unseen needle, piecing thought to act

and act to speech. They all exist within their own

estate, the mind, alive with what is here

today, the bars, the solitary

self, and all that isn't here—unless one falls

asleep, and then, exactly as the doctor said, the heart

has grown enlarged, it holds the river and its bridges,

children running, hiding, seeking, though not upon the grass

(forbidden), one who tags another screaming, "It". Those bodies

frozen by a touch, stone soldiers. No mother keeping watch

can guess inside each game exists the smallest act

of terror, only simpler, since they each are ended

by a summons to their private Eden, where all the table

is protected by the mother, who for reasons not disclosed,

has not been taken off to prison, and the father,

who has never once by day become the instigator

of another's pain. They are instead, themselves

one self, like arches holding up the bridge one child

or another runs across to find the square with towers,

steeples, statues seeming to bend down. The clock

with death each hour chasing life rings out

the time, and in between, one hears instead, "You may be free,

but you are small!" The playwright sees it all,

acts one to three—a stillborn birth—a lingering death,

a rising resolution to depart the graveyards and the cellars,

to take up pens and pencils, brushes, words, uncensored

life outside a ring of keys, hard dirt pressing down.

## Existential Law

The playwright sees it all: each reason to traverse
the stage (this table must be moved) is subtle
like a deer among the shadows hiding, but every act
is also bright as broken bits of sun that blind the teacher,
sweep the chalkboard clean of cold equations,
grammar, and even gild the students
row by row. Their faces light up like seraphim, their wings
too heavy for these awkward seats. They know more
than any chalkboard could contain, and come like strangers
from a near republic sent to offer reminiscence of a different
world. They need no passport or a stamp beyond
belief and disappear to jail or heaven. To the latter,
no adviser to the head of state can confess, except within
the private, weekend homes they've built inside themselves.

Only high on dark cathedral walls
where they've been carved in stone,
can they exist, such angels. Even those who've passed away are not allowed
to leave, or cross one border for another form. There is
no exit visa from existence. This place,
this time, does not allow the visitation
or departure of the unexpected. So call them
seraphim, since the secret, smug police are unfamiliar
with that name. They may see them glowing on the street,
but can't be sure exactly what they are. And if
one asks, does each one have the proper papers,

the carte d'identite for foreigners? They do,

although the glow obscures the face inside

the picture. Do they have the proper stamp to legalize

their visit? Although it's smudged, they do. Can we

arrest them for a glow, a beauty, or for wings

on wings? It seems one can't. Perhaps if one tries hard

a bylaw can be found. But for some who passed them on the bridge

or met one buying bread, there is some message better

than the bread, but not by much, if bread is all

there is. The message, not quite lost, is locked

inside the prison, and the playwright's free

to offer every mind it meets, not the jailer

but the jailed, scenes and visions, lines and light

that can be made from nothing more than what is circling

in one's head. Those friends found fit to be

let loose, have smuggled sentence after sentence out

and whispered them to others who believe

they can perform, without a shadow

being seen, this play that breaks a book

of laws like twigs, gathered up then snapped

across one's legs. Remember what the border guards and state

forget. The lion in its cage has never given up its crown.

# The Shadow of the Phantom King

Does anybody see the lion maned and standing
on two paws, released from locks and bars, the sharp claws
sheathed? His presence is itself the strength of claws and teeth.
Now is not that time. If like seraphim, one sees the shadow
of the lion on the stage or street, don't say but only
pray the one who casts the shadow will appear,
not just in paint, or paper, but in flesh
and fur. "Wrong, wrong!" The censor and interrogator
locking hands like London Bridge agree
on what cannot be said or seen. One may admit
how one has come to love the state, or else
one's wife; but never, not one word or hint, or shadow
of a word, no vision of desire, or regret
for freedom can be written or repeated. Not unless
the speaker wishes to surrender
all the world, to struggle through a sentence
of one's self crossed out. Right now
these words, his words, our words are secret,
but the secret is not silent. Soon like deer that are
and are not there, the state hears murmurs
that it must every tongue extinguish like flames,
must try to sever words from writer. Lock him,
unrepentant, somewhere deep and silent, left
to grow not more defiant, only mute
and crumbling into proper form. But judge and jailer
haven't learned, the needle must continue sewing.

Without a surgeon to remove or take apart
the brain, it just goes on creating sentence
after sentence, dark and light.

## Fate and Future

Asleep inside a cell the world grows large, or
rather wider, brighter than whatever, looking out
across the city from this hill, a child learns
to see. Everything below is small
like tiny blocks and cars, yet slowly turn your head
and see, as if it were a fan, the city spreading out
between two eyes, while just across the field, the castle
and cathedral rise as high as we ourselves.
Those who run the state from deep inside see
less than just one child hidden
in the bushes. Who's been given greater
vision? The child sees the sky, the river,
bridges and the castle too—those within it
only see the window's frame, a swatch of sky,
the bridges built along that side. Awake again
and drowning in that cell, the morning is another
wooden spar to keep one's self and hope afloat. Unseen,
the needle piercing thought to act (a child hiding on a hilltop)
and act to dream goes on. No surgeon
comes to take apart the brain, but sometimes
something delicate, a painted box appears
at breakfast. "Open. Open it," it cries. A message, "Hope
denied," is written in a lovely hand inside. A message
bigger than the box breaks all the rungs, destroys
the ladder one must have to clamber
up the side of any ship that stops to let one

climb at least part way above the depth

and sorrow of each day denied, the crow's nest

never reached, the border closed, the future

still unseen. Only words continue

to surprise, the way a lifeboat made

while drowning holds the almost given up, afloat.

## The Dissidence of Words

A week ago, a person hearing silence from that cell
might well have closed their eyes, stuffed their fists
inside their pockets, bit their lips, but now, too late,
too late. Too many people know the secret actions
of the playwright's mind, have seen them
dancing just behind the curtain
never opened, only lit like magic lanterns
from within. They've let their voices join the play.
Each one rises up in waves that flow beneath
the prison door and lift it; they flood beyond
the border gates, triumphant but afraid
because each voice has forced itself to face
and say, informant, sentence, judgment, silence,
dread injustice locked behind
closed doors, closed mouths, closed borders, banished,
banned; what if what they've named out loud
the hated, hidden actions of the state
aren't dead but wailing, watching
to deploy its tanks, its guns, its soul
against itself. Yet now is not that time; the lion
in its crown has been uncaged. The king
now walks at will through nervous, anxious crowds
unable to believe the cage they broke themselves
is gone. The king can wander freely down the hill
across the bridge that's almost older than all
the bodies buried in all the graveyards.

## The People

can destroy the state with just one song or else

refusal to comply. The state can free its people

with a single word. What does it take to talk

and feel the limits of one's self expand beyond

the pulsing of one's heart; the branching out

and living of one's thoughts confessed

after all that silence underground. All the borders

of the state are gone, yet won't the mind remember

where these were and thus remain confined? If not,

does this removal of the lines and bars, and wall, leave

livid scars behind? Perhaps they are the testament

to lives that have been kept restrained so long the brain

inside the skull is all the private self that's left. How does

it taste—the self outside? Does it taste exactly like this orange

without hands or numbers, pulp and seed and skin

all one? It tastes like all one ever knew to want—a life

without a guard, a censor, jailer, cell

or any further, deeper parts of hell.

# The Transformation of the Key

All beauty is a spoon of cheap aluminum
that's bent and twisted into something
like a spoon and something not,
but if one wished to make the simple, perfect
shape of spoon once more, one only need to press
coal-smeared fingers here and there
along that handle made of twisted metal
and there will be the spoon released to be itself, unless
it may have been so bent that just a small untwisting
breaks it, and you might hope that now there are
no laws to charge you just for seeking shape and purpose
pure and balanced in your hand. There are some

for whom it's not a spoon one uses
everyday, but those for whom the orange
hidden in their hearts has once again gained weight
and shape; all the whole, round skin says, "This is now
an orange of the world, not the just the mind. You may eat it
all, or save it, put it down, whatever you should choose
is yours to do, to hold one's freedom, not one's fate,
inside one's hand." The poet and the playwright choose
to offer every mouth and hand, a spoon, an orange,
and the words let loose like ringing keys that chime,
not just a few—but all, as if they were
a river bursting over rocks.

# Reply to an Unopened Letter

Received from the foreign streets
that coil themselves toward the market
square and widen to border
the Sava, I do not open
your hand folded envelope pasted
with two dinar stamps, in reply
to whatever questions may occur inside:

It is cold here; a gray roof slants
past my window. It seems I am well
though I cannot explain
why there is no connection
between your script and the neon loops'
fluorescent pink spelling, or the tricolored
code of the stoplight, followed
each night past the Jade. Of course now

I've unopened your letter so long
I imagine it's learning
to speak to itself, to decipher unwritten replies
to accuse me of having misplaced it,
of being forgetful, or simply ignoring
the simplest shapes of our own bodies. Buried
within this berserk geography of bed quilts
I study instead of your letter, I see ourselves

walking against the pebbled slope,

past the unrestored chapel. Your black bangs

sway with progression. Backwards

we gaze through its absent roof.

Wall stumps, weathered, surround

flagstones of grass. Below this

the mosques of the valley point

minarets up to the ruins left overlooking

noon-bleached expanses of red

tiled roofs, corrugated tiers

or sea combers. Here, it is cold;

a gray roof slants past my window. Where


have you hidden the delicate veins

of your wrists in these words?

## Embracing the Orange Hour

Isn't there a minute without hands
just these cool, green tables, marble; coffee
hot and sweet, one's breath blows circles
on the surface; sugar, sharp, rough grains slow
to melt; the tongue can feel
their many sides: the spoon some cheap aluminum
rebent to shape that makes a sound
against the glass, a sound that summons perfect,
towering clouds above the castle. The only castle
to discharge its dungeons, to elect the almost dying
prisoner king. See the small wind opening up
the flag that says the king of hearts not clubs
is here alive and safe inside. Stir the coffee—
now there is the song that rings no time but now
when friends, their scarves pulled loose and flapping
have arrived outside the window. In that one moment,
or the one before, they've stood stock still
across the street to string the swans and castle
clouds and coming spring together so they can't forget,
and time cannot devour what they love. The minute
when they cross the street and stop outside the window,
digging in their pockets to decide who owes the other
money; is there enough to tip the waiter? Do anybody's
pockets hold a pack of cigarettes? They have no watches yet
they know they are on time. Inside, among the cool, green
tables, there will be no time but coffee, friends

who've been away, the waiter who will work

no more than he desires. If there are any minutes here

each one is like an hour, or an orange eaten slowly

slice by slice when they are rarities you'd almost rather keep

than eat. Even just a fist of fragrant rinds

might tempt one not to die but wait

as everybody waits,

to greet the king who's scuffled down the hill,

across the bridge to sit here too

released from drowning in the sentence of the self

crossed out.

# The Open Door

is not enough for everyone. The music teacher's mother
not able to find comfort in the rise and fall of states
has hung herself at home with rope she's hoarded since
a shortage some years back. What to do? The music teacher
must come back and teach his students how to sing
forbidden songs and travel into other countries, anxious
to observe the fantasy of how a people once set free
might sing, but is that not the singing sung by you or me?
Or do the newly freed sing with greater passion, maybe, with
all border gates unlocked, one's smallest thoughts
no longer cross examined, once the people have destroyed the state.
Still, the mind, the mind may not agree. It may not find
this hour like an orange, or ever meet the king of hearts directing
people in the practice of becoming free.

There is, there always will be
one unable to accept the open door. That one
must be put outside the prison, yet brick by brick
and thought by thought this one will be, again, confined
within the pure, imperfect workings of the mind,
less free than unborn swans inside their shells, and blind,
the coffee cold, the waiter, never to return. For these
we must perhaps, give up the orange we have cradled
in our hands. Perhaps we have to peel this orange, careful
not to drop the rind, and having split apart
the pieces we must feed the disbelieving

citizens set free. How does it taste? —the taste
of prison keepers freed of prisoners, prisoners freed
from jail, the taste of borders breaking open
to allow free passage like a seraphim or swans
that swim from crumb to grass and down
and down the unencumbered river free.

# Crossing the Bridge

Its blackened statues rising up along each side
are not so old, but old enough to see some centuries
of kings thrown out through windows
high enough to break a neck, to crack a skull.
More ordinary bodies, if they were alive
when floating underneath one arch, could see
how symmetry creates, from stone to stone, one span,
another and a bridge appears above each bloated body,
all life's symmetry destroyed by death, yet crossing
through one arch that decimated
soul might hear, if it could hear,
the sainted and corrupt still walking back and forth,
supported by the beauty of the rising arches; each
side against the other leans, and those who came today
to linger on the bridge cannot believe the unimprisoned
king can walk here too, that he is free
to have the nails pulled out of each door,
hammered shut, to walk through every door
like this one where the cool, green tables welcome
poets who have waited years to sit and see again
the river, bridges and the castle reassembled like the scenery
behind a play, yet real. Midstream the swans no longer fixed
and motionless have paddled closer; clouds are drifting off;
the tower's clock still chasing death
with life says, "You are free to practice being free."

This is where the playwrights come to sit again and speak
outrageous thoughts out loud and write. It isn't
what it was before the tanks rolled in,
but those who sit here now are not
afraid of words, or thoughts, or acts. Their capital
is rearisen. There is nothing artist, actor, poet isn't
free to say, or to deny the beauty of the spiral
steps built narrow rock by rock from river up
to one small castle door through which one prayed
or wished to never be escorted. They are the stairs
to law and judgment, deafening, crumbling rooms
of logic gone awry. The handle, finally twisted
like a cheap and broken fork, won't work. A hammer
bends the courtrooms' and the prisons' keys which no one wishes
to reshape. Their locks as well are being beaten
never to accept another key. Just such small
destructions of the ever more distorted law, have left
that one door not unnailed but hammered shut. It's time
those laws are lost, some certain keys destroyed.
The rest still filled with the intent to open other doors
like this one where the green, cool tables wait to let the
people in. Their keys to home, not jail, to convents
turned to classrooms, none have given up their chiming
in the square, "We may be small, but we are free!"

.

## Epilogue

*Stand between the hunter and the hunted,*
*the hated and the hate—in that small space, imagine*
*God's compassion is our own, compelled to bloom,*
*or not, through all the tangled tendrils of the mind.*

## About the Author

TERRI ADAMCZYK earned her MFA at the University of Massachusetts Amherst, where she studied under James Tate and Dara Wier, among others. Her poetry and struggles with depression are the subject of a 2011 documentary by Stockton University Professor Jeremy Newman, viewable at vimeo.com/39163829. *The Amnesiac's Birthday* is her first collection.

Made in the USA
Middletown, DE
16 August 2021

45450188R00076